Sports can teach you so much about
yourself, your emotions and character,
how to be resolute in moments of
crisis and how to fight back from the
brink of defeat.

—*Arthur Ashe*

Caroline Lazo

Lerner Publications Company
Minneapolis

To Tyler

A&E and BIOGRAPHY are trademarks of A&E Television Networks, registered in the United States and other countries.

Some of the people in this series have also been featured in A&E's acclaimed BIOGRAPHY series, which is available on videocassette from A&E Home Video. Call 1-800-423-1212 to order.

Lerner Publications Company
241 First Avenue North
Minneapolis, MN 55401

Website address: www.lernerbooks.com

Library of Congress Cataloging-in-Publication Data

Lazo, Caroline Evensen.
    Arthur Ashe / Caroline Lazo.
      p.   cm.   —   (A & E biography)
    Includes bibliographical references and index.
    Summary: Traces the tennis career of Arthur Ashe and describes the discrimination he faced as he worked to master "the white man's game."
    ISBN 0-8225-4932-8 (alk. paper)
    1. Ashe, Arthur—Juvenile literature. 2. Tennis players—United States—Biography—Juvenile literature. [1. Ashe, Arthur. 2. Tennis players. 3. Afro-Americans—Biography. 4. Discrimination in sports.]
    I. Title.
    GV994.A7L39   1999
    796.342'092—dc21
    [B]   97-38737

Manufactured in the United States of America
1 2 3 4 5 6 – JR – 04 03 02 01 00 99

CONTENTS

Chapter **ONE**

THE STUFF OF DREAMS

SUMMER IN ENGLAND IS USUALLY A QUIET TIME, BUT in July 1975 London's Heathrow Airport was one of the busiest places in Europe. People streamed in from all over the world to attend the famous tennis tournament at nearby Wimbledon. Fans were eager to see defending champion Jimmy Connors, who was on a winning streak, destroy Arthur Ashe. "The match was supposed to be a slaughter," Arthur remembered, "and I was to be the sacrificial lamb."

Arthur faced the match as he faced everything in his life—studiously, calmly, carefully. The younger Connors was ready for Arthur's famous hard-hit balls. But knowing Connors's weakness, the low forehand approach shot, Ashe decided to go wide on both sides with his serves. When returning Connors's serves, Arthur would chip the ball down the middle so Connors couldn't blast it back. If Connors came in to the net, Arthur would calmly lob the ball back. Sending him "junk" balls would confuse him, Ashe thought, and for the most part, they did.

Arthur won the first two sets, 6–1, 6–1. Connors won the third, 7–5. Although Connors led 3–0 in the fourth set, Arthur, always cool under pressure, won six out of the next seven games to win the match. Once again, Arthur was the top-ranking player in the world.

Ashe's strategy, preparation, and finesse on the court helped him beat Connors.

Connors and Ashe shook hands after Ashe won the men's singles title.

Wimbledon. The U. S. Open. The French Open. The Australian Open. To aspiring tennis champions, those names are the stuff of dreams. They are the most prestigious tournaments in professional tennis. And Arthur Ashe—the first black man to gain prominence in the sport—won them all. But it was his personal code of behavior both on and off the court that made Arthur so respected around the world. Even under great stress, his cool demeanor was legendary—and sometimes criticized.

As a young boy growing up in Richmond, Virginia, a part of the segregated South, Arthur learned a lesson

Arthur spoke about his career in front of many groups after his retirement from competitive tennis. Here, in 1992, he talked to high school students about tennis and answered questions about HIV, a deadly virus he contracted from a blood transfusion in 1988.

he never forgot. His father taught him that in order for a black boy to succeed in "the white man's game" (tennis), he must study harder, work harder, and behave better than the white players. It is no wonder that the frail, skinny boy, whose tennis racquet looked bigger than he did, poured his heart and soul into the game he loved and became an outstanding student at the same time. He had to do these things to succeed. Yet even when he was accepted by whites in his community, he was always aware of the contempt that many of them had for blacks. It formed "a shadow," he said, that followed him wherever he went.

Between 1968 and 1980, Ashe won thirty-three events. In 1975 he was the number-one ranked player in the world, and in 1985 he was elected to the International Tennis Hall of Fame. After retiring from competitive tennis, Ashe organized tennis clinics in poor urban areas and tirelessly protested racial intolerance in the United States, in South Africa, and around the globe.

Ashe was convinced that the causes he fought for as an adult stemmed from his childhood experiences. "The core of my opposition to apartheid," he wrote, "was undoubtedly my memory of growing up under segregation in Virginia." Hints of his success as a tennis champion could be found there, too. When we look at the roots of his family tree, planted centuries earlier in Africa, his success seems even more amazing, his life even more remarkable.

Chapter **TWO**

OUT OF
SLAVERY

IN **1735, 167** SLAVES WERE HERDED ONTO THE **HMS**
Doddington. They were held captive on a long voyage
from West Africa to America, where they were traded
for tobacco—a prized commodity in Europe. One of
the young Africans, known only as "slave girl," was
bought by Robert Blackwell, a rich tobacco farmer. According to early family records, she was Arthur Ashe's
first ancestor in America. "I have tried to imagine the
terror, rage, and fear of my nameless ancestor," Ashe
reflected, "born free, captured and transported to a
strange and brutal world . . . by masters who could not
imagine that blacks were human beings."

Blackwell's slave girl would spend the rest of her life
in slavery on the farmer's Virginia plantation. Eventu-

13

ally the young slave married. The couple took the name of their master (Blackwell) for their own—a common practice on Southern plantations—and raised a family on the farm. By the time Abraham Lincoln's Emancipation Proclamation was issued in 1863, five generations of Blackwells had been added to the family tree. When Everett Ashe, a bricklayer and carpenter, married Amelia Johnson, a Blackwell descendant, the Ashe branch of the family began to grow. It was from one of their seven children, Arthur Robert Ashe, born in 1920, that Arthur Ashe Jr. got his name.

Though the Thirteenth Amendment to the Constitution had officially ended slavery in the United States, blacks felt anything but free. To preserve white supremacy in the South, states passed new laws to ensure segregation of blacks. Segregation became prevalent throughout the region—in everything from restaurants and trains to schools and swimming pools.

Blacks who defied the "Whites Only" signs posted at facilities such as public bathrooms and playgrounds or who otherwise dared to challenge white authority could expect midnight visits from the Ku Klux Klan. Klan members—local white businessmen, farmers, politicians, and others—cloaked themselves in hoods and white sheets, crept into black communities, and vandalized homes and property. They sometimes beat, kidnapped, and murdered black "offenders." Relatives found their loved ones strung up on nearby trees. These lynchings, the Klan hoped, would warn blacks

Ku Klux Klan members in the South tormented African Americans—especially those who tried to exercise their rights as free and equal citizens.

A company advertised its discrimination policy on the side of the building.

to stay in their place—where they would remain secondary to whites and observant of white authority.

Because whites owned the major businesses in the South, most blacks had no choice but to work for them. Not all white people were racist, however.

In Richmond, Virginia, various white employers did hire Arthur Ashe Sr. for a number of jobs. Skilled in carpentry and auto mechanics, he was a hardworking, disciplined man and always—almost always—focused on his work. One day, while doing laundry for one of his employers, Arthur Ashe Sr. saw Mattie Cunning- ham hanging her laundry on clotheslines next door. He introduced himself, and they became friends and soon fell in love.

In 1938 Arthur and Mattie were married. Five years later, on July 10, 1943, in Richmond's only black hos- pital, Mattie gave birth to the couple's first child, Arthur Robert Ashe Jr. When Arthur Jr., as his family called him, was four years old, his brother Johnnie was born. Even as toddlers, the boys were shown by their father's example how to survive in a world dom- inated by whites—not by defying them but by match- ing them in intelligence, knowledge, skills, and honesty.

Chapter **THREE**

AT HOME ON THE COURT

AS A YOUNG BOY, ARTHUR JR. WAS SHY AND, according to one of his aunts, looked "small and pathetic." He was too small for most sports—especially football, which his father refused to let him play. But he loved baseball and idolized Jackie Robinson, the black player who, like boxing champion Joe Louis, broke the color barrier in his sport. When Robinson joined the Brooklyn Dodgers, Arthur said, "Every black man, woman, and child in America became a Dodger fan."

In 1947, a pivotal year for Arthur, his father was appointed special policeman for Brook Field Park, an eighteen-acre park in one of Richmond's largest black neighborhoods. The job was particularly prestigious for a black man, and Arthur's dad was thrilled to get it. But no one was more thrilled about his father's new position than Arthur, because working at Brook Field meant living there, too. The new family home would be a small house at 1610 Sledd Street—right in the middle of the playground. Young Arthur Ashe was all of a sudden surrounded by baseball fields, swimming pools, and four tennis courts. "The event changed my life," he recalled later. When Arthur entered kindergarten, the usual what-to-do-after-school question never arose in the Ashe household.

Although Brook Field was not a particularly beautiful park, it provided African American kids with a place to play and practice sports.

But in 1950, tragedy struck the family. Only twenty-seven years old, Arthur's mother suffered complications during her third pregnancy and died following surgery. His last memory of her was a pleasant early morning at home. She was wearing a blue corduroy bathrobe as she stood by the door, waiting for Arthur to finish his breakfast. He remembered hearing some birds singing in the oak tree outside. That image, he recollected later, "burned itself into my memory."

Though not quite seven years old when his mother died, Arthur would always remember the empty feeling that he kept to himself—a sort of secret sadness that stayed with him all of his life. This feeling may have accounted for the words often used to describe Arthur as an adult—such as cool, aloof, and detached. But at the time of his mother's death, Arthur's main concern was his father. The loss of his wife devastated Arthur Sr., and he didn't hesitate to express his feelings in front of his sons. The boys had never seen their father cry before, and their only wish was to make him feel better and to make up for the terrible void in his life.

Arthur's grandmother explained to her eldest grandson that his mother had gone to heaven. "Your mother is gone, Arthur Jr.," she told him. "She's gone to heaven." When Arthur asked where heaven was and if he would ever see her again, his grandmother assured him that if he was a good boy, they would meet again in heaven. "Then," she told Arthur, "you can stay with her forever and ever." Those words from his grandmother and the strict but compassionate behavior guidelines set by his father shaped Arthur's life. Always at the back of his mind was a longing to see his mother again. He missed the way she read to him and how she praised him when he learned new lessons at school.

The death of his mother was traumatic for Arthur, yet 1950 was also a year of discovery for the young boy. Because of his small build, Arthur played games and sports in which height and size were less important than quickness and agility. Even at the age of seven, he excelled in baseball and basketball. Then one day he saw Ron Charity, Richmond's best black tennis player, practicing his serve on a court just outside the Ashe house. "You play tennis?" Ron asked Arthur, who had hit only a few balls at the playground. Shy and awestruck by the champion player, Arthur couldn't answer. But when Ron asked him if he would like to *learn,* Arthur ran over to the park's equipment box that sat outside beneath his bedroom window, picked out a racket ("a twelve-dollar nylon-strung [racket]," he later recalled), ran back to the court, and said, "Yes."

"As casually as that," Ashe later wrote, "my life was transformed." He had discovered tennis and was determined to learn the game. His immediate goal was to hit the ball over the net and seventy-eight feet down the court—a lofty goal for a seven-year-old who weighed just fifty pounds. But Arthur had always been

Ron Charity, who introduced Arthur to tennis, went on to become the number-one ranked player in the country.

a quick learner, and he soon mastered the basics of tennis. The more tennis Arthur played, the less time he spent on the baseball diamond. When he wasn't returning balls across the net to Ron, he spent hours at a time hitting them against a backboard. During the following few years, he worked on his stroke, his form, and his timing.

To Arthur, timing became "the most important element in tennis." By the age of ten, he began to focus on combining his natural agility, speed, and good coordination with a sense of timing—timing produced not only with his hands but with his feet. The eyes, too, were crucial to timing. "At 120 miles an hour, a

tennis ball can elude the best eyes," he wrote. "From the beginning, I had no trouble waiting for just the right moment. Because of my lack of size and weight, however, I had to develop a semi-lob off the forehand as a form of survival." Ron taught Arthur the Eastern forehand grip, which was "like shaking hands with my [racket]," he explained. Ron told Arthur that it was the best grip for a beginner. "The hand is firmly behind the [racket] handle at the moment the ball touches the string," Arthur later reflected. The grip, he said, was "a good starting point for future experimentation."

As long as Arthur played tennis at Brook Field or on the few other playgrounds where blacks were allowed, he could have fun and feel good. But, as Ron Charity knew, if the young player wanted to excel in the sport and to play in major tournaments one day, tennis would not be all fun and good feelings. Tennis, Arthur would discover, was known as a white man's game—not just in Virginia, but throughout the world.

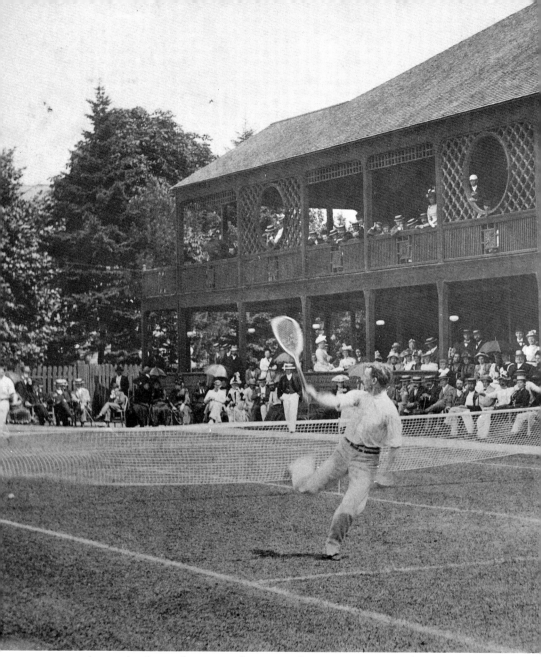

In the early days of tennis, players and spectators were almost
exclusively rich white people.

Chapter **FOUR**

THE WHITE MAN'S GAME

TENNIS ORIGINATED IN ENGLAND AND WON GREAT popularity in 1877, when the first Wimbledon tournament took place. Traditionally enjoyed by British royalty and upper classes, the game derived from earlier racquet-and-ball court games that emerged in France as early as the twelfth century.

In the United States, tennis was played primarily at private country clubs whose membership automatically excluded blacks. For a black person to even set foot on a country club tennis court in the 1940s and 1950s, especially in the heart of America's segregated South, was unheard of—unless he was there to clean it.

One day in 1953, while Arthur practiced his forehand during a break in the Central Intercollegiate Athletic Association's tournament at Brook Field, the event's director spotted Arthur and told Ron Charity that he would like to meet the boy. Dr. Robert Walter Johnson, the director, was a medical doctor from Lynchburg, Virginia, who believed that good health depended on a combination of a strong mind and a strong body. In developing young black tennis players into the best they could be, Dr. J—as everyone called him—practiced what he preached. Once an All-American football player and later a tennis advocate, he—like Arthur's father—followed a strict code of conduct and passed it on to the young athletes.

After he was introduced to Dr. J, Arthur returned to the court and continued to play. He sensed Dr. J, Ron, and Arthur Sr. watching him as they huddled in conversation. Arthur felt excited, as though something special was going to happen. And it did. After the tournament, Johnson invited Arthur to spend part of the summer at his home, where he trained a select group of black tennis players. Both Arthur and his father were overjoyed. And Ron Charity felt especially proud.

For Arthur, the chance to train under Dr. Johnson was like a miracle. He would continue his summer training with Dr. J for seven more years, developing his natural skills in the process. Only when he was told to change his backhand did a conflict arise. He had used the standard backhand, which Ron Charity had taught him, and didn't want to change it. But when Dr. Johnson called his father, and his father

Dr. J trained Arthur and other talented African American kids to play competitive tennis.

made a special trip to talk to his son, Arthur listened to him as he always had. "Dr. Johnson is teaching you now, Arthur Jr.," his father told him. "You do what they say." Arthur complied, although he said later that he didn't change his grip that much.

While staying at Dr. J.'s, Arthur traveled to black tournaments around the area and was excited to see the growing number of black tennis players in the South. But he saw them only where they were allowed—in black communities, never in white ones. Though the U. S. Supreme Court ruled in 1954 that segregation in the schools was unconstitutional, segregation continued to permeate the Southern states.

When Arthur traveled by bus, he had to sit in the back, in a section marked off by a white line. Many restaurants and churches barred blacks from entering. "Even where we were not barred, we were not welcome," he later recollected. "I grew up aware that I was a Negro, colored, black, a coon, a pickaninny, a nigger, an ace, a spade, and other unflattering terms."

Though the shadow of prejudice followed him throughout his youth, the lessons Arthur learned from his father and mentors always propelled him forward. To conquer the white man's game, Arthur was told that blacks must outshine the whites, both on and off the court. They must engage—and never enrage—their white opponents. Other rules, "meant only for little black Southern boys," were mandatory for the few black children qualified to compete with whites. Arthur would have to abide by them all:

- When in doubt, call your opponent's shot good.
- If you're serving the game before the change of ends, pick up the balls on your side and hand them to your opponent during the crossover.
- Make sure your behavior is beyond reproach.

Black boys didn't dare challenge the second-class status imposed on them by white players. But how long could they stifle their anger and their hurt feelings? "It would be years before I understood the emotional toll of repressing anger and natural frustration," Arthur recalled later.

Meanwhile, Arthur Sr. had taken on the role of both

mother and father—as he had promised Mattie he would. But five years after his wife's death, he met Lorene Kimbrough and married her. "My memories of Mama were strong," Arthur recalled, "but I knew there was no alternative when Daddy said . . . 'I'm getting married.'" Only eleven years old, Arthur didn't feel ready for a stepmother—and a stepbrother and stepsister as well. But Arthur and Johnnie both became close friends with their new step siblings, Robert and Loretta.

A housekeeper, Mrs. Berry, helped to manage the Ashe household. Yet it was Arthur Sr. who set the rules, did the disciplining, and even used a leather strap (if only for a second) to enforce proper behavior. If the children had no special appointment or outside school project, they were expected to be at home. "No hanging around" was at the top of Arthur Sr.'s list of rules.

Arthur Sr. instilled in his children self discipline, a strong work ethic, and the drive to succeed.

Arthur Sr. followed his own rules, too. He was greatly admired in the black community. He gave up smoking and he drank little. He was as thoughtful toward others as he expected his children to be, and although he himself had only an elementary school education, he insisted that his children get the most complete education available. When Arthur Sr. made the rounds of the Brook Field playground, he often took his boys with him—making sure they learned the responsibilities of an important job. He told Arthur Jr., "I can show you how to paint, fix cars, work with tools, plan ahead. I can also show you that when I don't have anything special to do, I'm at home." To survive in the white man's world, he always said, one had to keep on top of things and accumulate as much knowledge as possible.

Arthur and the other children in the Ashe household had chores to do, ranging from cutting wood for the fireplace to feeding the dogs to studying for school. Unlike some of their friends, the Ashe children weren't paid for doing household chores or earning good grades. To them, these were simply part of life's duties. Besides, Arthur knew that his father had had to borrow money to buy a set of encyclopedias for him, so there was no way the young student could expect any money from his father. But when Arthur saved enough newspapers to fill a truck, he sold them at a center that bought them by the pound and was allowed to keep the money he earned. Also, he was allowed to keep old copies of *National Geographic* he found. He loved the magazine because through its pictures he could travel around the world—something he dreamed of doing someday.

Arthur's extended family was always an important part of his life. Here he poses with his wife, Jeanne, daughter, Camera, and other family members.

Ever mindful of the importance of education, Arthur would later return to Richmond to appear in schools and talk to students.

Arthur loved to read, because reading took him far away from Richmond, thanks to his growing collection of *National Geographic* magazines. He also loved gospel music and the history behind it. "My grandmother used to tell me that some of the black elders in her youth would gather in a circle for what they called a 'ring-shout,' accompanied by the beating of a drum in a slow, steady cadence as the elders slowly shuffled about, releasing their rage and frustration in music and dance," Arthur once reflected. "I hear those sounds, that rage and that beauty, in gospel music."

His grandmother's love of music furthered Arthur's interest in the Bible, which he began to read in his youth. The link between music and religion would always remain strong in his mind. Playing the trumpet, he later recalled, reminded him of Joshua, "whose trumpets made the walls of Jericho fall down," and of Gabriel, "whose trumpet would announce the end of the world and the coming of judgment day." As a sixth-grader at Baker School, Arthur was already president of the student council. He looked forward to new and bigger challenges in junior high—to play the trumpet in the school band and to play tennis wherever he could.

Althea Gibson, Zina Garrison, and Arthur Ashe posed for a photo at Wimbledon in 1990. Gibson, the first African American to compete in the world's top tennis tournaments, won both the All-England Championships at Wimbledon and the U. S. National Tennis Championships at Forest Hills in 1957 and in 1958. Competing at Wimbledon in 1990, Garrison made it to the finals, losing ultimately to Martina Navratilova.

Chapter **FIVE**

THE TORCH
IS PASSED

WHEN JACKIE ROBINSON BROKE THE COLOR BARRIER in baseball, eager black athletes throughout the country were ready to follow in his footsteps. But when Althea Gibson began to play in major tennis championships in 1950—becoming the first black person to do so—there was no one waiting in the wings, no one to pick up the torch, until Arthur Ashe came along a decade later. Althea was twenty-four when she began to play in major tournaments; Arthur was twelve.

Though Arthur was on his way to becoming the nation's best young black tennis player, he took nothing for granted and worked harder than ever. Ron Charity took him to the Richmond Racquet Club to watch the pros play, and he was particularly impressed by Pan-

Pancho Gonzales rested after winning the National Men's Indoor Tennis Championship in 1949. At the age of twenty-one, he was the number-one ranked amateur player in the country.

cho Gonzales. Arthur wanted Gonzales's autograph but was too shy to ask for it. Arthur also continued to spend part of each summer with Dr. J, gearing up to play against white junior players.

By the age of twelve Arthur was ready for tournament play. He entered—and won—the ATA National Singles (Boys) title in 1955, and repeated his victory in 1957, 1958, and 1960. But the going was not all smooth. In 1960, during the Middle Atlantic Junior Championship in Wheeling, West Virginia, Arthur became a victim of blatant racist behavior.

"As happened much of the time when I was growing up, I was the only black kid in the tournament," Arthur remembered. When he left for Wheeling, Arthur was prepared, he thought, for signs of racism. But when some of the white players trashed and destroyed

Arthur (far right) *and his doubles partner, Hubert Easton* (second from right), *shook hands with their opponents before a match in the Eastern Junior Tennis Championships in 1959.*

one of the cabins on the premises, Arthur was shocked. When they blamed *him* for the crime, his shock turned to anger. Arthur denied that he had been involved, yet the white boys stuck to their false story, and local newspapers even published it. Arthur's main concern was his father's reaction upon hearing the news. But when Arthur called his father in Richmond, Arthur Sr. asked only one question: "Arthur Jr., all I want to know is, were you mixed up in that mess?" When Arthur said he wasn't involved, the questioning quickly ended. "He trusted me," Arthur said. "With my father, my reputation was solid."

A spotless reputation was of crucial importance, Arthur Sr. had always told his son. Arthur Jr. took his words to heart. "I have tried to live so that people would trust my character. . . . Sometimes I think it is almost a weakness in me, but I want to be seen as fair, honest, trustworthy, kind, calm, and polite," Arthur later wrote. "I want no stain on my character, no blemish on my reputation."

The incident in Wheeling proved just how difficult it was to have such high standards in a hostile world, but another situation in 1960 gave him hope. While in Charlottesville, Virginia, for the National Interscholastics, a few white players asked Arthur to go to a movie with them. Arthur was sure that blacks wouldn't be allowed in the theater, so he declined the invitation. But when the others insisted, he went along. Arriving at the ticket booth, the boys were told that

Arthur would not be admitted—only white people were allowed. Arthur would never forget the boys' reaction. "Well, if he can't go in, none of us will go," one of the boys told the ticket agent. They all left the theater. The actions of peers like these helped Arthur stick by his goal—to compete in and master the "white man's game" of tennis.

In order to compete with other players around the country—especially those from California—Arthur would have to play tennis all year, not just in summer. But in Richmond, no indoor courts were available to black tennis players. The problem was solved when a friend of Dr. J.'s invited Arthur to live with him and his family in St. Louis, Missouri, where he could enter the senior class at Sumner High School. Richard and Jane Hudlin and their son, Dickie, welcomed him warmly.

Arthur was thrilled to discover that at Maggie Walker High School in Richmond, he had already completed some of the courses required of seniors at Sumner in St. Louis. So he had more time to devote to tennis—which he did.

First, he had to learn to play on a wooden floor and to adjust his strokes to the new surface. Arthur practiced on the wooden floor in the St. Louis Armory. The floor, he discovered, made an important difference. "A wooden floor is fast and slick, balls skid off the floor and accelerate after the bounce," he wrote. "I had to shorten my backswing to play well."

Arthur forehanded a shot across the net during the National Interscholastic Tennis Championship in 1961.

On the clay courts in Richmond, he would remain behind the baseline and wait for the ball. But in St. Louis he learned to drop back a yard or so, then charge the ball. He worked on a topspin backhand in St. Louis, as well. In the process, Arthur's grip changed, too—from the Eastern to the Continental grip. Using the Eastern grip, he had to rotate the racket to shift from a forehand to a backhand shot. Though it wasn't as secure as the Eastern, the Continental let him "hit everything with the same grip"— forehand, backhand, volley, and serve.

All of his new strokes and strategies served him well, as he proved by winning his first United States Lawn Tennis Association national title, the National Junior Indoors, in November 1960. He had more reason to be proud the following month when J. D. Morgan— the tennis coach at the University of California at Los Angeles (UCLA)—offered him a scholarship. UCLA and the University of Southern California (USC) ranked at the top of the list of schools for tennis in the United States. By the end of his senior year in high school, Arthur ranked fifth in the country among junior players and had become a member of the Junior Davis Cup team.

Arthur ranked high among the girls, too, at school and tennis events. Though he and his friends usually went out in groups, he "flipped" over more than a few girls—and one in particular. While at an ATA event in Stamford, Connecticut, Arthur met—and later became

UCLA campus

engaged to—Pat Battles. "My crush on Pat Battles lasted eight years," he wrote. They broke up when Arthur decided that there was too much to see and do—too many "new worlds" to visit—before settling down in marriage.

Arthur had become famous for being a "first"—the first black to win a UCLA scholarship; the first black to be a Junior Davis Cup player; the first black to win the International Scholastics; and many more. Though he was proud of breaking down racial barriers, and of often being the first to do so, it was, he said, "an indication that we still had far to go." He was still playing in clubs where the only blacks in sight were either weeding the gardens or parking the cars.

Arthur was glad to move to Los Angeles, where liberal attitudes prevailed over racism and an exciting world of tennis awaited him at UCLA. His mentors and coaches—his father, Ron Charity, and Dr. Johnson—had trained him well, and he was ready for a new adventure.

Ashe talks with J. D. Morgan, his tennis coach at UCLA.

Chapter **SIX**

TURNING
POINTS

ARTHUR HAD PLANNED TO STUDY ARCHITECTURE AT UCLA, but his new mentor and coach, J. D. Morgan, advised him to study something less demanding of his time so he would have more time for tennis. Arthur also had to allot time for Reserve Officers' Training Corps (ROTC) duties, because every male freshman and sophomore was required to enter the program.

For his major, Arthur chose business administration, which he thought would be a valuable asset in his later years. While attending UCLA on scholarship, he was required to work 250 hours a year keeping the tennis courts in good condition. Arthur never complained about the responsibility. He welcomed the chance to show his appreciation for the scholarship. To him, California was paradise—with its swaying palm trees, warm ocean breezes, and year-round sunshine.

Only a few weeks after his arrival on campus in the fall of 1961, Arthur faced a major decision. The Balboa Bay Club in Orange County had invited the UCLA tennis team to play in its annual tournament. But J. D. Morgan was told that Arthur would not be allowed to participate because he was black. The news saddened but didn't surprise Arthur. He had grown up with racism.

J. D. told Arthur that if he decided to make an issue of the blatant discrimination, the team would stand with him and not play. A big man, he had large hands and an even larger heart. "We don't have to send the team [to the Balboa tournament]," the coach told Arthur. "It's up to you."

It was a turning point in Arthur's life. The questions multiplied in his mind: If I make an issue, will all the other clubs ban me, too? Will my tennis career be over? Am I prepared to follow through with a total commitment—with a full-time effort to fight racial prejudice?

Arthur remembered his father's advice—to succeed in tennis, Arthur must become an example of excellence, a proven champion, so that one day the sport would no longer be for whites only. He decided he was not ready to battle racism so early in his college tennis career. Coach Morgan agreed with Arthur's decision not to protest the club's rules at that time and to concentrate on his tennis. Morgan also said that

Arthur was excited to be playing for UCLA, and he worked hard to excel.

Dinah Shore, who befriended Arthur in Los Angeles, was an avid golfer as well as a tennis player.

when Arthur was more established, he would be "in the position of fighting them" on his own terms.

The Balboa incident hardened Arthur's attitude toward private clubs, but he was not bitter. "Many clubs treated me kindly," he wrote. Hosts of the famous Racquet Club in Palm Springs, for example, gave him a standing invitation to play there. Dinah Shore—singer, movie star, and tennis player—invited Arthur to play on her tennis courts whenever he wanted to. Though Arthur never played there, he did play mixed doubles with her and others at the Beverly Hills Tennis Club.

Arthur liked the way Dinah played tennis—for pure enjoyment, with no concern for the score. She loved to have fun. "I've heard . . . that you can tell someone's personality by the way they play tennis," Arthur once said. "[Actor] Sidney Poitier is as silky on the court as he is on screen, and [actor] Rod Steiger has a brutish first serve that goes with the type of characters he plays." As for Arthur himself, he was as studious on the court as he was in the classroom—always with a new idea or strategy on his mind.

The Beverly Hills Tennis Club, located in the heart of America's movie industry, attracted top tennis players from all over the world—including Arthur's childhood hero, Pancho Gonzales. When Arthur saw Gonzales practicing at the club, he was overjoyed. The

Pancho Gonzales continued to play professional tennis well into the 1970s.

veteran player watched Arthur hit a few balls, and a new friendship began. Arthur joined Gonzales on the court from time to time as the veteran player's practice partner. Arthur felt an immediate kinship with Gonzales, in part because he, too, had dark skin. "I don't know if it was because I was black or polite, but he took a liking to me and helped me refine my serve," Arthur remembered. Gonzales emphasized use of the body—not the arm—when serving. "If you serve with your arm, you'll get tired," he warned Arthur. Arthur saw the same thoroughness in Gonzales's serve as he found in J. D. Morgan's coaching. He was grateful for the chance to benefit from their examples.

Coach Morgan was always there for his players— even off the court, as Arthur found out one Christmas. During a break from school in his sophomore year at UCLA, when most of the students went home for Christmas vacation, Arthur had run out of money. He was too proud to tell anyone about it—especially his father. With not even enough money to see a movie in nearby Westwood, he felt sad and alone. Morgan invited Arthur to join his family for Christmas, but Arthur felt he would be intruding on a family gathering, so he turned down the invitation. He told Morgan that he had made other plans—although he had not. Yet Arthur felt better knowing that his coach had thought to include him with the Morgan family.

That Christmas break was one Arthur would never forget. On Christmas Eve he had just enough money to get a sandwich out of a vending machine in the basement of the dorm, and he spent the evening alone in his room. The experience taught him a lifelong lesson. "I wasn't tempted to run out and steal anything," Arthur said, "but I thought long and hard about what it meant to have no money at all for an extended period. I was determined never to be in that situation again."

Arthur was one of the few students who was happy when the holidays ended, classes resumed, and the cafeteria reopened. Most of all, he was eager to get back to tournament play.

Chapter **SEVEN**

OLD
MEMORIES,
NEW
CHALLENGES

ALTHOUGH **A**RTHUR **STUDIED HARD AND PRACTICED** his tennis as often as possible, he also enjoyed getting together with good friends and attending dances in the dorms. Still shy around female classmates, he did build longlasting—and sometimes challenging—friendships.

Once when Arthur was attracted to a young woman "across the dance floor," he summoned up the nerve to introduce himself and dance with her. Struck by the contrast of her "coal-black hair and white skin," he could not resist getting to know her. Back in Virginia, he recalled, he could have been killed for pursuing such a relationship. But California colleges were more open, and girls seemed to be drawn to athletes, no matter what their color. In his later published writings, Arthur referred to his new girlfriend as Phyllis Jones, a fictitious name, to protect her privacy. Phyllis was the first white girl Arthur had ever danced with or dated. They enjoyed discussing their different backgrounds and their views of the country's racial problems. Arthur was impressed by her intelligence.

Through dating women from different backgrounds, Arthur learned about cultures other than his own. "I learned about Asians from dating Asians, I learned about Jews from Jewish girlfriends," he reflected. But his relationship with Phyllis was cut short. Although she had told her parents she was dating a member of the UCLA tennis team, she had not told them he was black. When the team appeared on television and her parents saw Arthur for the first time, they were enraged. The girl's mother, Arthur reported later, was devastated. "I don't ever want him in my house!" she had screamed. The dating ended there. Memories of Richmond and its "Whites Only" signs flooded Arthur's mind. The shadow of racism, it seemed, would never leave him.

But good luck followed Arthur, too. After he and his friend Charlie Pasarell played an exhibition at the California Club, one of the club's members, Joan Ogner, praised Arthur's playing and asked about his future plans. He said he hoped to be able to go to Wimbledon that summer, though, at the time, the plan seemed like an impossible dream. After raising money—on the spot—from other club members, the woman handed

Charlie Pasarell, Arthur Ashe, J. D. Morgan, Dave Reed, and Dave Sanderlin

Arthur the money for the trip to London. "You deserve it," she told him. People like that, Arthur realized, kept up his spirits and helped him fulfill his goals.

The London suburb of Wimbledon is famous because of the tournaments played there at the All-England Lawn Tennis and Croquet Club. Surrounded by high brick walls covered with ivy, the Centre Court reminds American visitors of New England's Ivy League campuses. But to understand the Wimbledon mystique, Arthur believed, tennis players should know about its past—especially the way it rose from the ashes of World War II to regain its premier place in the world of tennis. During that war, sports writer Allison Danzig described the scene in a report to *The New York Times:*

> Wimbledon . . . where the Queen sat in the royal box when strawberries were in bloom; where the fashionables gathered for the crowning event of the social season; where the finest lawn tennis players from the world over experienced a feeling of exaltation just to step out on the immaculate turf of the center court, groomed to fastidious perfection—the Wimbledon of all this swank, ivy and tradition is now a nursery for pigs . . . commandeered for the war's duration to help keep England's meat basket full while submarines fill the waters formerly used to transport the pigs from Denmark.

The sound of hard-hit balls zooming across the net had been replaced by "the fury of bombing planes," Danzig reported. Bombs left the royal box in ruins and the competitors' stand in shambles. "Will the day ever come," he asked, "when enemies will gather in the camaraderie and good sportsmanship of a world tennis championship? Will there be another Wimbledon?"

No one appreciated that part of Wimbledon's history more than Arthur Ashe. Ever since Arthur's childhood—and his first glimpse of *National Geographic*—he had been fascinated with the far-off lands and historic sites described in the magazine. And, in the summer of 1963, no place interested him more than Wimbledon. To Ashe, Wimbledon's fall and rise seemed to symbolize the defeats and comeback victories of those who played there. By the 1950s, Wimbledon had again regained the elegant and hallowed carpet of turf it had before the war. To picture it as a

Overview of the courts at the All-England Lawn Tennis and Croquet Club, Wimbledon, England

Ashe backhanded the ball in his match against Chuck McKinley at Wimbledon in 1963.

breeding ground for pigs with bombs bursting over-head seemed impossible for Arthur to imagine.

Arthur was thrilled to reach the third round at Wimbledon. "I was so excited I could hardly contain myself," he later recalled. But he eventually lost to Chuck McKinley, the United States's top player. But Arthur analyzed the loss in his typical, honest way. "I was talented but inexperienced," he concluded. He was grateful to have played there at all—and especially grateful to Joan Ogner, the California Club member who made the trip possible. Though he lost, he knew he had played well. He also knew he would work even harder to return for another Wimbledon.

More comfortable now in the world of competitive tennis, Arthur felt less of the racial prejudice that remained prevalent in other parts of society. The world of sports, he said, was like a cocoon that shielded him from the growing unrest of the civil rights movement in America. Competitions in Europe also kept him focused on tennis and distracted him from events at home.

After Wimbledon, Arthur traveled to Budapest, Hungary, where he made it to the semifinals in a tournament. Though he lost to Torben Ulrich—a world-renowned player on clay courts—Ashe's reputation as a rising star spread quickly around the globe. By the end of the summer he was ranked as the sixth best tennis player in America. "The summer of 1963 was . . . very good for me," Arthur recalled.

Chapter **EIGHT**

OVERCOMING THE PAST

ARTHUR'S CROWNING MOMENT IN **1963** CAME when Bob Kelleher, captain of the United States Davis Cup team, invited him to join the team. Aside from the national tennis championships, played at the West Side Tennis Club in Forest Hills, New York, the Davis Cup ranked as a "major star in my sky," Arthur later stated. Named after Dwight F. Davis, who donated the original silver cup, the championship circuit aimed to "stimulate international competition and to promote goodwill," Arthur wrote. For Arthur, the invitation meant the opportunity to travel around the world and to gain invaluable experience playing tennis. Making the Davis Cup team also meant he had achieved a goal he had set for himself years earlier:

Segregation and racism had made me loathe aspects of the white South but had left me scarcely less of a patriot. In fact, to me and my family, winning a place on our national team would mark my ultimate triumph over all those people who had opposed my career in the South in the name of segregation. . . . I saw my Davis Cup appointment as the outstanding honor of my life to that point. Since no black American had ever been on the team, I was now a part of history.

Around the same time he became a member of the Davis Cup team, Arthur had to make another big decision. Because he was in such good physical shape, Arthur knew that he would be drafted into the army following graduation. After completing his sophomore year at UCLA, Ashe had to decide whether to continue in the ROTC program, which would mean officers' training upon graduation. He consulted with his father—still his most trusted mentor—about getting drafted or electing to stay in UCLA's ROTC program.

"He liked the idea of me becoming an officer," Arthur said of his father. But before he finalized his decision—to be drafted and fight in the Vietnam War or to stay in the ROTC—Arthur consulted with his tennis coach, J. D. Morgan, who had served in World War II, and Davis Cup captain Bob Kelleher. Both agreed with Arthur's father and advised Arthur to stay in the ROTC.

Members of the U. S. Davis Cup team in 1965 included (clockwise from far left) Coach George McCall, Marty Riessen, Dennis Ralston, Frank Froehling, Arthur Ashe, and Clark Graebner.

Arthur also sought the advice of his brother Johnnie, then a Marine Corps officer in Vietnam. He agreed with the others. Johnnie thought Arthur could best serve his country by excelling on tennis courts around the world—in places where blacks had seldom been allowed. In doing so, he would encourage and inspire other blacks and help to awaken the white world at the same time.

Although he felt confident that the ROTC was the right choice, Arthur was still haunted by certain questions. He wondered if black soldiers would resent his playing tennis and enjoying himself while they were risking their lives on the battlefield in Vietnam. He wondered if his country would consider him a coward for not going overseas. While they respected boxing star Muhammad Ali for refusing to go to war for religious reasons, would they lose respect for Arthur, whose religion played no part in his decision?

After much careful thought, Arthur decided to stay with the ROTC. But he would always regret not having been in the war. "I view my escape from the war as one of the great omissions of my life," he later reflected.

Arthur went back to UCLA for his junior year in the fall of 1963. By the start of the 1964 season, he was the top player at UCLA and the sixth ranked amateur in the nation. Although some people continued to criticize Arthur for not speaking out or actively participating in the civil rights movement, he did support Dr. Martin Luther King's nonviolent protests to end the segregation of blacks in America. King had awakened the conscience of the country in the late 1950s and 1960s. Other more militant activists failed to win Arthur's sympathy, however. "One consequence of my commitment to reasoning and reconciling," he acknowledged, "would always be to have some people think of me as conservative or opportunistic, or even a coward. So be it." By pursuing his own goals and by proving that blacks could excel on the tennis court as well as whites, Arthur hoped to encourage other blacks to pursue such goals. At the same time, he listened to his critics and began to wonder if he should be doing more.

When he returned to UCLA in the fall of 1964, Arthur witnessed for himself the growing protest against racial injustice in the country. He listened to

Dr. Martin Luther King

the speeches of Martin Luther King, Senator Robert Kennedy, and Andrew Young (who later became U. S. Ambassador to the United Nations), and began to develop his political views. "I felt myself wanting to open up more and more about the way our society

By 1965, Ashe was the number-one ranked college tennis player in the country.

operated," Ashe reflected. But he also knew that he must graduate from college and represent the United States in Davis Cup matches.

In 1965 Arthur won the National Collegiate Athletic Association (NCAA) singles and doubles titles (with Ian Crookenden) and became the top-ranked college tennis player in America. His picture appeared on the covers of major magazines, including *World Tennis, Life,* and *Sports Illustrated.* Arthur wanted to squeeze another trip into his busy schedule. He told Bob Kelleher that he would feel honored to go with the Davis Cup team to Australia, although that meant postponing his graduation from UCLA until 1966. So in the summer of 1965, Ashe traveled to Australia with the rest of the team, with his plans for graduation in spring 1966 and his post-graduation ROTC military obligation firmly in place.

"Australia turned out to be as important to my tennis career as meeting Dr. Johnson and living in St. Louis during my senior year in high school," he later declared. For the first time, Ashe had the chance to play on grass courts for three months in a row, and to make a name as an international player.

Arthur won four tournaments in Australia and made it to the finals in two others. He also learned that there was more to life "than hitting balls back and forth across the net." Arthur made many friends in that remote country—including some of the Aborigines with whom he felt a special bond. He discovered that

they, like blacks and Indians in the United States, were considered second-class citizens by a white majority.

Learning about other cultures had always fascinated Arthur, and traveling with the Davis Cup team nourished that longtime interest. But 1966 brought other new events to Arthur's life as well. February 4, 1966, was designated "Arthur Ashe Day" in his hometown of Richmond, Virginia. The town that had barred him from tennis tournaments because of his color now honored him for his achievement in the sport. Arthur felt no special allegiance to Richmond, but he knew his father did. If the day made his father proud, that was all that mattered.

Ashe came away from Australia with some big wins (opposite page). *He was welcomed home to a celebration in his honor in Richmond* (above).

Chapter **NINE**

"WELL DONE, SON"

ARMED WITH A BACHELOR'S DEGREE, ARTHUR FELT confident about the future and looked forward to more tennis and to building a career in business one day. But in 1966, at the age of 23, he headed for ROTC training camp in Fort Lewis, Washington. From there he went to the United States Military Academy at West Point, New York, where he worked as a data-processing officer and as assistant to the tennis coach, Bill Cullen.

Balancing both jobs was a challenge. In addition, Arthur continued to play tennis, although the stress of so many obligations kept his overall performance down. Still he won the U. S. Clay Court Championships in 1967, racked up many singles victories for the

Davis Cup team, and by the end of that year became the number-two ranked amateur player in the country. "This time," he reflected, "Charlie Pasarell was ahead of me. . . . I knew I would have to try harder, but weaving a delicate path between my roles as Lieutenant Arthur Ashe, U. S. Army, and Arthur Ashe, tennis player, demanded total commitment."

Ashe talked with Charlie Pasarell during the National Indoor Championships in 1967.

Davis Cup captain Donald Dell

In February 1968, the United States Tennis Association (USTA) appointed Bob Kelleher—the former Davis Cup captain—as its president. In March the International Tennis Federation (ITF) "opened" tennis—allowing professionals and amateurs to play together. Arthur's friend and trusted advisor, Donald Dell, became captain of the Davis Cup team. Donald shared Arthur's strong feelings about segregation in the United States and apartheid in South Africa, and their shared desire to fight both became a fundamental part of their friendship.

That same year, Arthur's balancing act, between his army duties and tennis, became trickier—and riskier. He added Arthur Ashe, social activist, to his prestigious profile. Dr. Martin Luther King and his thousands of followers were going to jail for sitting in restaurants reserved for whites only and for entering whites-only churches. They were arrested for sitting in the front seats of buses where only whites were allowed to sit and for countless other peaceful protests against segregation of blacks in America. By this time a role model for black people everywhere, Arthur Ashe decided to speak out. "The status quo would not do," he said.

So when Reverend Jefferson Rogers, a friend of Dr. King, asked Arthur to speak at his church in Washington in March 1968, he agreed to do it. "I accepted his invitation," he later wrote, "knowing it was against [army] regulations. . . . but I accepted rebuke as my way of paying dues to the cause. After all, I had done nothing in the '60s but play tennis and enjoy life." Yet he confessed: "I was more nervous about my speech than any tennis match I had played."

Arthur told the congregation that blacks must rise up and take responsibility. He encouraged them to follow the examples of athletes like Jackie Robinson in baseball and Boston Celtics star Bill Russell in basketball. He said that blacks had to show the world who they really were and put to rest the myths that blacks were inferior and passive. "With self-confidence and a desire to help others, the black athlete, whether of average ability or a superstar, must make a commitment to his or her community and attempt to transform it," Arthur declared.

Rather than attack white society, Arthur hoped to encourage self-esteem and common purpose among blacks. His speech was neither militant nor rabble-rousing, but it made headlines in the *Washington Post*. "Ashe Becomes Activist" and "Negro Tennis Star Emerges from Shell," the newspaper announced.

Arthur's superiors at West Point were not happy. Arthur was warned "not to make any more speeches of even a vaguely political nature." He was not surprised at the army's reaction. After all, army officers must be above politics. Further protests would have to wait until he finished his military service.

In April 1968, soon after Arthur's speech, Martin Luther King was assassinated. Two months later, Senator Robert F. Kennedy, then a presidential candidate as well as an important civil rights leader, was assassinated. The tragic losses of King and Kennedy drove

Robert F. Kennedy

Although he did well in other tournaments in 1968, Ashe fell to Rod Laver in the semifinals at Wimbledon.

Arthur to go all out in his tennis—to do the best he had ever done to honor his dead heroes. "I had a two-month winning streak, which was quite unusual in those days," he told **PBS** journalist Charlie Rose.

In the summer of 1968, Arthur had to carefully plan his leave time from West Point to play in the first U. S. Open tournament. One week before he arrived in Forest Hills for the big event, Arthur won the men's singles title at the U. S. National Championships in Brookline, Massachusetts, making him the top-ranked amateur player in the United States. He was clearly on a winning streak and wanted it to last. There were two special reasons Arthur wanted to play his best in the Open, and they were sitting in the stands waiting to cheer him on. His father and Dr. Johnson—Arthur's favorite fans—had flown to New York for the tournament.

West Side Tennis Club, Forest Hills, New York

Arthur easily won his first two matches at the Open, and he went on to beat his third round opponent—Roy Emerson—in straight sets. In the quarterfinals, Arthur beat South Africa's Cliff Drysdale. He went on to beat his Davis Cup teammate Clark Graebner in the semifinals. Arthur's opponent in the championship match would be the talented Tom Okker, a player from the Netherlands who had registered as a professional. In addition to his hope of winning a major title, Tom was eager to win money as well. But Arthur was equally motivated—to win his biggest tournament yet.

Though Tom Okker was a formidable opponent, Arthur was in his best shape for the event, and he was ready to win. He had been following a weight-training program at West Point, which allowed him to beef up. Also, he had been running twenty minutes a day and practicing with tennis pros Gene Scott and Dick Savitt in New York during the weeks prior to the event.

Okker's quickness served him well against Arthur in that historic championship. He won the fourth set 6–3, tying the score at two sets apiece. Fifth sets can be pivotal, however, as Arthur explained. "Fifth sets of tennis matches separate the great from the good. It clearly defines a player's level," he said.

So, as the fifth set began, Arthur felt confident. Having won twenty-four straight singles matches, he was at his peak. "'If I just hold my serve,' I told myself, 'I'll win.'" Donald Dell kept reminding him of the basics—get your first serve in; don't miss your first volley;

Ashe's endurance led him to beat Tom Okker in the finals of the U. S. Open.

make your opponent miss before you do; don't give away the easy points by making unforced errors. Dick Savitt called to Arthur from the stands, "Bend your knees, kid! Bend your knees!" At 6-foot-1, Arthur felt a little uncomfortable crouching to return a serve.

At 30–40 in the seventh game, Arthur decided to take real advantage of Okker's weak backhand, serving three consecutive balls to Okker's weak side and winning the game. But Okker hung on. The score was 5–3 in Arthur's favor, and Arthur had to hold serve one more time to win the match. Arthur went for the ace and got it. Then he forced Okker to miss another backhand shot. Finally, Ashe rushed the net and leveled a volley past Okker for the win. Okker "waved his [racket] helplessly at my last forehand volley," Arthur

With his father at his side, Arthur Ashe Jr. awaits the final ceremony after winning the men's singles title of the first U. S. Open in 1968.

said. The finest moment came at the award ceremony, when his father stood by his side with tears in his eyes and whispered, "Well done, son."

The following week Arthur appeared on the CBS television news show, *Face the Nation.* He was the first athlete ever to appear on that program. Arthur grabbed the chance to talk about the rising momentum among black athletes as a result of recent civil rights legislation.

Fresh from his victory at the U. S. Open, Arthur prepared to go with the Davis Cup team to Australia—this time to win back the silver cup for the United States. "I had to play Ray Ruffles, who was on a winning streak," Ashe later recalled. Ruffles was left handed, so Arthur had to move to the left to stop his opponent from swinging his serve so wide. "I moved to my left to return serve and went for the lines whenever I had an opening," he said. His strategy worked, and he won in four sets. As the reality of the victory sank in, Arthur recalled "sitting in the dollar seats as a twelve-year-old in Richmond, watching the Aussies play."

Ashe's dream of a team win also came true. "All the hours and days of travel, practice, strange hotel rooms, aching shins and elbows had converged at this point," he later recalled. "It was worth it. We had won the Davis Cup."

The team returned to the United States via Southeast Asia so they could play some matches for the forces in Vietnam. Almost immediately, Arthur saw

Ashe and his Davis Cup teammates gather with President Richard Nixon in the White House to admire the trophy the team had won for the United States.

the effects of the war that had aroused such passions at home. "We were stunned by what we saw . . . men who had lost their eyes, part of a face, arms or legs. We saw jaws wired shut or eyes closed and greased to keep the lids from fusing shut." Arthur was more convinced than ever that the war was a tragic and unnecessary loss of young lives. Looking back, he called Dr. King's early opposition to the Vietnam War courageous and correct.

Arthur's travels around the world opened his eyes to human achievements as well as human suffering. He saw great art and listened to great music, and was forever moved by both. "Without either," Ashe remarked, "life would be dry and without feeling." Recalling the music of different countries, certain instruments stood out in his mind—trumpets in England, violins in Austria, pianos in France, flutes in the Middle East, drums in West Africa. "Each sound is like the signature of a place and its people," he wrote. "Each is a part of the harmony of the world."

Arthur helps run a tennis clinic for young people in Washington, D. C.

Chapter **TEN**

CONFRONTING THE SHADOW

NOT ALL COUNTRIES WELCOMED ARTHUR ASHE WITH open arms. South Africa, where apartheid and the second-class status of blacks were established ways of life, did not. In 1969 Ashe applied for a visa to travel to South Africa to play tennis. Not until 1973 was his visa finally approved by the South African government. In the meantime, Ashe and his supporters succeeded in having South Africa banned from Davis Cup play.

As he arranged to compete in the 1973 South African Open, Arthur was aware that South Africa had been trying to improve its image so the country would be allowed to participate in the 1976 Olympics. He demanded three conditions from the South African government—that the audiences not be racially segregated, that he not be made an "honorary white," as had occurred with other famous blacks visiting South Africa, and that he be allowed freedom of speech and the freedom to travel wherever he pleased. Arthur saw his visit to South Africa as an opportunity to encourage young blacks there to work toward freedom.

Some people wondered why Ashe didn't devote the same effort to promoting civil rights in his own country. Arthur saw the circumstances differently. "The conditions for black people were much worse [in South Africa] than in the United States, and I was

Urban blacks in South Africa were forced by law to live in townships such as Soweto, a sprawling shantytown outside of Johannesburg. The country's largest city and industrial center, Johannesburg was the site of the 1973 South African Open.

A bench in Johannesburg, South Africa

personally being denied an opportunity to play in a tournament that, rightly or wrongly, was a part of the international circuit. I felt I should have the right to play in this tournament or the tournament shouldn't have the right to be included in the ITF circuit."

At the South African Open, Arthur lost to Jimmy Connors in the men's singles final, but he won the doubles title with Tom Okker. Yet it wasn't the tennis that Arthur remembered most about South Africa. "I looked apartheid directly in the face there," he reflected.

"Whites Only" and "Non-whites Only" signs greeted Arthur everywhere in South Africa, reminding him of his childhood in Richmond, Virginia. "I saw the sneer of superiority on the faces of many whites . . . and despair on the faces of the blacks." He would never forget the young black boy who followed him around Ellis Park in Johannesburg, the site of the Open.

Arthur finally asked the boy why he was following him. The boy answered, "Because you are the first truly free black man I have ever seen." The boy's answer made Arthur happy, because Arthur had shown by example what a black man could achieve—but also sad, because segregation of blacks was so pervasive in South Africa that freedom to a young boy seemed impossible there.

Other blacks in South Africa criticized Arthur for playing tennis in the first place. "Nothing I said made any favorable impression on those desperate young blacks," he later said. Despite the despair, Arthur was pleased that he could serve as a role model in South Africa, where role models for blacks were usually found in prisons for opposing apartheid. Nelson Mandela, who has spent all of his adult life fighting for freedom for blacks in South Africa—while in jail and out—was a hero to Arthur.

Arthur's opposition to apartheid in South Africa led to his involvement in TransAfrica—a think tank for African and Caribbean affairs run by black members of the U. S. Congress. The organization was directed by one of Arthur's childhood friends from Richmond, Randall Robinson. Arthur also became a founding member of Artists and Athletes Against Apartheid. The group's goals were to discourage athletes and entertainers from playing and performing in South Africa and to put pressure on South Africa to abolish apartheid and acknowledge equal rights for blacks.

Demonstrating against apartheid in front of the South African embassy in Washington, D. C., are (left to right) *Rory Kennedy, Randall Robinson, Douglas Kennedy, and Senator Gary Hart. Rory and Douglas are the children of the late Robert F. Kennedy. Randall Robinson heads the organization TransAfrica.*

In 1974 Arthur became president of the Association of Tennis Professionals (ATP). He also became a consultant to a number of foundations and to tournament sponsors such as Aetna Life and Casualty and Philip Morris. (Eventually, as smoking and health problems

became linked scientifically, the alliance of the tobacco industry and sports events bothered Ashe
deeply.) Critics in the media began to say that Ashe
was spending too much time on business ventures and
social causes. They questioned whether his tennis was
suffering as a result. Finally, the media asked if Arthur
had reached his peak. Though he admitted he was
spreading himself pretty thin, he would never agree
that he had reached his peak in tennis—and he decided to prove it.

Recalling his successful weight-training program at West Point prior to the 1968 U. S. Open, Arthur and a few friends—including long jumper Henry Hines—went to Puerto Rico for intense conditioning. Footwork was a chief priority. "Foot-eye coordination is more important in tennis than hand-eye coordination," he declared. "The hands and arms don't forget how to swing the [racket], but the feet were another problem. Anybody can swing a [racket]. It's the great feet that win Grand Slam titles."

When the World Championship Tennis (WCT) season began in 1975, Arthur's foot-eye coordination worked perfectly. He beat Bjorn Borg in the WCT finals in Dallas and was feeling good. The only problem was a chronic pain in his left heel, which caused Arthur to walk with a limp until a warm-up relieved it. "Aging," Arthur reasoned, as his thirty-second birthday drew near.

Encouraged by his Dallas victory and his Australian Open triumph in 1970—both won on grass courts—Arthur was ready to return to that "hallowed carpet of turf" called Wimbledon. So, in June 1975, Arthur packed his bags and left for London—and the biggest match of his life.

Chapter **ELEVEN**

A LONG WAY FROM BROOK FIELD

NO ONE WAS MORE CONFIDENT OF WINNING AT
Wimbledon than Jimmy Connors. He was ranked
number one in the world, and Arthur was seeded
(ranked) seventh that year. Ashe and Connors would
go head to head in the finals at Wimbledon.

To prevent the "slaughter" that was predicted by the
media, Arthur consulted with his advisers and came
up with a new strategy to throw Connors off his
game. "I had never tried it on a grass court before,"
he told Charlie Rose. The strategy was "to take the
speed off the ball and give him a lot of junk, as we
call it, because Connors is a good counter-puncher.
The harder you hit it, the better he likes it." It was
important, Arthur said, to keep the ball down the mid-

Ashe (above) *and Connors* (below) *fought for the men's singles title at Wimbledon in 1975.*

dle of the court, draw Connors to the net, and lob to Connors's backhand.

Although Connors won the third set and was leading in the fourth, the pressure finally got to him. Arthur won six of the next seven games. "When I took the match point," he wrote, "all the years, all the effort, all the support I had received over the years came together." He had won "the most significant singles match of the seventies," as Arthur later wrote. Arthur Ashe had become the first black athlete to win both the U. S. Open and Wimbledon. Not even his idol, Pancho Gonzales, had won at Wimbledon!

Ashe receives his trophy.

Arthur signed copies of his book Portrait in Motion *for fans in 1975.*

Arthur had come a long way since the day he first saw Gonzales but was speechless and much too shy to ask for his autograph. He had come an even longer way since that day at Brook Field park in Richmond, when Ron Charity asked him if he would like to learn to play tennis. But Arthur's win at Wimbledon carried new responsibilities. Sponsors such as Catalina sportswear and others clamored for his endorsement, and fans mobbed him wherever he went. His exhibition fees doubled after the Wimbledon triumph. So did the demands on his time and on his speaking engagements. No longer could Arthur feel free to speak out whenever and wherever he felt like it. He had learned that if he spread himself too thin, his tennis would suffer. So, in his typical, controlled and thoughtful way, Arthur sought the perfect balance between all of his activities, making sure that his tennis clinics for children received top priority.

Arthur won five more tournaments in 1976, but his most memorable event of the year happened on October 14 in New York. That day he met Jeanne Moutoussamy, a graphic artist at a television station. They

Arthur and his girlfriend, photographer Jeanne Moutoussamy, goof around with a camera.

chatted while she was photographing him at a fund-raising program for the United Negro College Fund.

Even before they met, Jeanne had a premonition about Arthur that was later revealed by her friend Carol Jenkins. "She said to me, 'You know I'm going to marry Arthur Ashe.' I laughed because she had never met him. And of course when they did, they fell in love immediately."

Arthur was attracted to Jeanne's heritage. She was part African American and part East Indian. Above all, she was "bright, articulate, and sensitive," he later said. It was Jeanne who helped him talk about his mother, about the effect her death had on his life, and about how the tragedy had drawn him closer to his father. When Arthur's father met Jeanne, he was stunned by the resemblance to his late wife. "Just like your mother!" he told Arthur. Arthur liked to surprise Jeanne with a red rose now and then—just as his father used to do for his mother. Arthur was certain that the memory of his mother helped to bring Jeanne and him together. They were married in 1977, and Arthur's friend, United Nations Ambassador Andrew Young, performed the ceremony.

In the late 1970s and early 1980s, Arthur was plagued by injuries—including foot problems and eye inflammations. His sponsors began to lose interest in using him as a symbol. But Arthur faced such adversity with characteristic courage. He wrote a biweekly column for the *Washington Post,* worked as a sports

In February 1977, Arthur and Jeanne were married at the United Nations Mission in New York City. Arthur was walking with crutches after undergoing an operation on his heel.

commentator on TV, conducted clinics, and continued to play tennis—although his playing had become inconsistent. When he failed to qualify for the Grand Prix Masters in 1979, after losing to John McEnroe in Australia, Arthur began to think about retirement. His strenuous, nonstop way of life had finally caught up with him.

In July 1979, after conducting a clinic for underprivileged children in New York, Arthur suffered a heart attack. Six months later, he had quadruple coronary bypass surgery. Undaunted, Arthur continued to pursue his interests—off the court. He knew his competitive tennis-playing days were over. But his writing, business consulting, and tennis clinics continued at full speed. His retirement also marked a beginning—the beginning

With a wide grin, Arthur shows off his scar following open-heart surgery.

As captain of the U. S. Davis Cup team, Ashe conferred with John McEnroe during a break in McEnroe's match.

of his term as captain of the U. S. Davis Cup team. During his years as captain (1980–1985), Arthur learned more about his strengths and weaknesses than he had ever known before. He also learned more about other players—such as the notorious tennis star John McEnroe.

As captain, Arthur came face to face with John McEnroe many times. McEnroe's quick temper and foul language were legendary. "McEnroe was difficult to take at times," Arthur recalled. "As captain, I was for protocol; he was not," Arthur stated in his typical, understated manner. In fact, no two men could have been more opposite in their behavior. Critics could not understand why Arthur refused to lay down the law when McEnroe yelled obscenities at fans and officials alike—for all the world to hear.

Though Ashe did get angry, he restrained himself. A line from a poem by John Dryden came back to him: "Beware the fury of a patient man." But later Arthur did ponder his refusal to fight fire with fire. "I wonder," he recollected, "whether I had not always been aware, at some level, that John was experiencing my own rage, my own anger, for me, as I never could express it." Also, Arthur had developed a genuine respect for McEnroe's character and integrity. This respect, said Ashe, "defused my outrage at behavior so different from my own."

By 1983, Arthur had co-authored several books—*Advantage Ashe; Arthur Ashe: Portrait in Motion;* and *Off the Court. Arthur Ashe's Tennis Clinic,* an instructional book, was published in 1981. He continued to write, and in spite of another bypass operation in 1983, he made more public appearances. Arthur became a spokesperson for the American Heart Association and accepted honorary doctorate degrees from some of America's leading colleges—LeMoyne-Owen College, Dartmouth College, Princeton University, Saint John's University, and Virginia Union University.

But the "honor of a lifetime," as Arthur called it, came in 1985 when he was inducted into the International Tennis Hall of Fame in Newport, Rhode Island. All of Arthur's family—including Jeanne and her parents; his father and stepmother; his brother Johnnie and his wife, Sandra, and their daughter, Luchia—joined him there.

His father's presence at the event reminded Arthur once again of the many miles he had traveled since his early days in Richmond, Virginia, when racism had ruled him out of tournaments and cast a lasting shadow on his life. But at the moment—on that special day at the International Tennis Hall of Fame—there was sunlight in the shadow, and Arthur had put it there.

Among other items on display at the International Tennis Hall of Fame in Newport are articles, photos, and Arthur's shoes and racket from his 1975 Wimbledon victory.

Members of Artists and Athletes Against Apartheid held a press conference at the United Nations building in New York City. Pictured (from left to right) are Tony Randall, Arthur Ashe, Ruby Dee, Randall Robinson, Ossie Davis, and Harry Belafonte.

Chapter **TWELVE**

FROM WORDS TO ACTIONS

HAVING RETIRED FROM COMPETITIVE TENNIS, ARTHUR felt free to turn his words into actions against racial discrimination wherever it existed. As 1985 approached, it still existed in South Africa in full force. On January 11, 1985, Arthur joined forty-six others—including teachers, state representatives, the president of Rutgers University, and others—to protest the pro-apartheid position of South Africa's government in front of its embassy in Washington, D.C. The protesters were handcuffed, arrested, and jailed.

Anticipating the arrest, Arthur had called his father in Richmond to warn him of the event before it happened and before the *Washington Post* and other news media could report the protest. Arthur's father told him, "Do whatever you think is right." As always, having his father's support and trust was important to Arthur. Although he went to jail, Arthur felt satisfied that turning his words into action helped to bring about the release of anti-apartheid protesters from South African prisons—some of whom had been imprisoned for twenty years. Arthur later explained the importance of his standing up for justice that day at the embassy. "I believe that I was destined to do more than hit tennis balls. The abrupt end of my tennis career only accelerated my search for another way I can

Ashe and other protesters were arrested at a demonstration outside the South African embassy in 1985.

make a contribution. I don't want to be remembered mainly because I won Wimbledon."

Arthur's family was the center of his life. No matter how many hours Arthur spent on planning public demonstrations, he always made time for family. Arthur also made time for writing and reading his favorite books. "I have always been in love with the English language and the power of the pen," Arthur reflected. His uncle, Horace Ashe, recalled, "Even as a young boy . . . when the other boys were playing marbles or other games, he'd be sitting, looking at some book, asking what's this word or that word." Arthur shared his love of reading with Jeanne. They both loved Maya Angelou's poems. They liked to read poetry, biographies, and many other types of literature.

Shared experiences of all kinds bound Jeanne and Arthur together, but one stood out above all the rest— the birth of their daughter, Camera, on December 21, 1986. "When he talked about her, his face would light up like stars," Horace Ashe said. The family moved to Mount Kisco, New York, away from the noise and the trendy restaurants surrounding their apartment on the Upper East Side in Manhattan. Although it was easier to raise a child in the country, Jeanne missed the vitality of New York City.

In 1988 Arthur was hospitalized in New York for a brain infection. A battery of tests performed at that time revealed he had AIDS. Doctors believed Arthur had contracted HIV, the virus that causes AIDS, from a blood transfusion he had received after a heart operation in 1983. Arthur took the news calmly. In fact, he later told Frank Deford, a friend and sports journalist, that having AIDS was "not nearly as trying as being black." When asked if he would pray for his recovery, Arthur answered with typical candor and grace, "God's will alone matters, not my personal wants or needs. When I played tennis, I never prayed for victory in a match. I will not pray now to be cured of heart disease or AIDS."

The following year, Arthur received the terrible news

Arthur faced everything in life—good and bad—with strength.

With Jeanne's support, Arthur spoke at a press conference in 1992. He announced to the public that he had AIDS.

that his father had died of a stroke. "My heart withstood the shock," he recalled, "but I cried and cried when I heard the news. Dominating, stern, protective, my father had loved me and taken care of me when I needed him the most."

Arthur's father had also instilled in him a respect for the truth. When people asked him why he just didn't lie about the AIDS discovery, he reminded them of his father's words: "Don't hide anything; tell the truth." Although Arthur had hoped to delay the announcement as long as possible for the sake of his family's privacy, he couldn't stop others from leaking it to the press. He finally announced the news publicly on April 8, 1992. In so doing, he became an inspiration to countless others around the world who had contracted the dreaded virus.

Despite the illness, Arthur wasted no time in pursuing his many activities—including the creation of inner-city tennis programs for young people in Newark, New Jersey; Detroit, Michigan; Atlanta, Georgia; Kansas City, Missouri; and Indianapolis, Indiana. Arthur also established the Arthur Ashe Foundation for the Defeat of AIDS. "I was conscious of the possibility that I did not have sufficient time left to mount such a project, but I became determined to move ahead with it, come what may," he said. Unlike other AIDS projects, Arthur's would be global in scope, because AIDS, he reminded audiences, "knows no boundaries."

Upbeat and optimistic, Arthur focused on the positive aspects of his life from then on. He enjoyed increasing international acclaim for his most comprehensive literary project, *A Hard Road to Glory: A History of the African-American Athlete,* published in 1988. "The project was a natural," he told the *Chicago Tribune.* "It brought both sides of me, the bookish and the sports-minded, together. Once I made the decision to do it, I had to go at the book the way I've always done things—the way our teacher at Maggie Walker High School insisted upon—all out with everything I've got."

Arthur, Jeanne, and Camera finally moved back to New York City to be closer to the New York Hospital–

Jeanne, Camera, and Arthur Ashe took a break during the Arthur Ashe AIDS Tennis Challenge in 1992. Money raised at the benefit went to the Arthur Ashe Foundation for the Defeat of AIDS.

Cornell Medical Center where Arthur received expert care for both heart disease and AIDS. But he never let his physical condition interfere with his social causes. In fact, on September 9, 1992, he flew to Washington, D.C., to speak out against America's treatment of Haitian refugees and to march in front of the White

Ashe was arrested at a demonstration in September 1992.
Demonstrators were protesting the U. S. government's decision
to turn back Haitian refugees during a conflict in Haiti.

House on their behalf. Ashe joined more than 2,000 others who were willing to be jailed for their peaceful protest. Freed after paying a fine, he returned to New York—feeling good for having helped bring attention to the plight of the Haitians.

Friends often asked Arthur why he worked so hard—when his health was so at risk—to seek freedom for blacks around the world. Maybe, he replied, he was "making up for not doing more" in the early days of the civil rights movement in America. "I am sure I will never know with full understanding why I held back from the fray when I did and why I plunged into the fray, in my own fashion, when I did," Arthur reflected. "All I know is that I have tried at all times to do what I thought was right and appropriate, and that sometimes the effort to do right, and above all, not to do wrong, led me into inaction."

Perhaps most important to Ashe himself was the impact he had on children—from the underprivileged boys and girls in South Africa to the poverty-stricken young people in Haiti to the children of AIDS patients in New York. To all of them he was living proof of courage in times of crisis and of hope in times of sadness.

Arthur Ashe was honored as the Sports Illustrated *Sportsman of the Year* in December 1992.

Chapter **THIRTEEN**

A TRUE CHAMPION

ARTHUR **A**SHE **NEVER COURTED HONORS, AWARDS,** or special recognition of any kind. In 1992, however, honors were heaped upon him. Arthur received the Helen Hayes Award, the National Urban League Award, the first annual AIDS Leadership Award of the Harvard AIDS Institute, the American Sportscasters Association Sports Legend Award, and the Sportsman of the Year award by the editors of *Sports Illustrated* magazine. He was both surprised and happy, and his spirits were lifted—momentarily, at least.

Arthur was hospitalized in 1993 with the deadly *Pneumocystis carinii* pneumonia (PCP), a virus that attacks many AIDS patients with weakened immune systems. It was not the long list of awards that brought him peace of mind then, but family love, friendships, and fond memories. One memory in particular—of a vacation in the Bahamas with Jeanne and Camera—was on his mind as he rested in his bed. He recalled that special family time with Arthur Rampersad, a good friend and the co-author of Arthur Ashe's final memoir, *Days of Grace*.

> We were under the stars, the hour was late . . . and Camera was still up, but what did we care? She was happy after a day in the sun and the sea, and now she was dancing to the music of a calypso band with a little friend she had just met. Jeanne was happy, too, talking easily with the wife of a musician she had met earlier. . . . As I sat in an armchair watching my little daughter dance and my wife's face sparkle with life, a wave of emotion like one of the waves of the ocean a few feet away from us washed over me. . . . My joy was that I was there, on that beach under those stars listening to that music and watching the two people I loved more than anyone or anything else in the world, and I did not want that feeling of perfect joy ever to end.

Arthur's physical condition worsened, and on February 6, 1993, he died of pneumonia at New York Hospital–Cornell Medical Center. More than 11,000 people attended Arthur's memorial services in New York and in his hometown of Richmond, where he was buried

Reverend Jesse Jackson spoke at a funeral service for Arthur Ashe on February 10, 1993.

next to his mother. Jesse Jackson, among other noted speakers, praised Arthur's character and code of conduct. Arthur's close friend, sports journalist Frank Deford, captured the essence of the champion. "In the end, the outpouring of emotion we gave to him spoke selfishly to our hope—that if we could not save his life, what he stood for might help to save us.... He was, I came to think, in matters of race, the Universal Soldier, some kind of keystone figure we need if ever brothership is to triumph."

Not everyone at the services was famous. Children from Arthur Ashe's tennis clinics were also there. To them, Arthur was a model of athletic excellence. Yet, as he often reminded them, athletic excellence may be the key to winning matches, but it is only a small part of being a true champion.

POSTSCRIPT

On July 10, 1996, a twelve-foot bronze statue of Arthur Ashe was unveiled in the athlete's hometown of Richmond, Virginia. The dedication ceremony was preceded by months of argument over the statue's placement on Monument Avenue, where Robert E. Lee and other Civil War heroes who fought to preserve slavery are honored. Arthur's brother, Johnnie, addressed the issue when he told the 1,500 people at the ceremony that "Arthur Ashe Jr. is a true Virginia hero, and he belongs." Former Virginia governor Douglas Wilder noted that Monument Avenue "was now an avenue for all people."

There was no argument, however, when the new

The Arthur Ashe monument (left) *aptly shows him with children. In addition to being a great athlete, Ashe was a teacher at heart. The Arthur Ashe Stadium* (opposite page) *hosts the annual U.S. Open.*

Arthur Ashe Stadium in Flushing Meadows, New York, was dedicated on August 25, 1997. The state-of-the-art building amazed a crowd of 22,500 who attended the opening ceremony to the U.S. Open. Don Budge, Jack Kramer, Boris Becker, John McEnroe, Billie Jean King, Chris Evert, Martina Navratilova, Monica Seles, and Steffi Graf were just some of those who came to honor Ashe and the building named after him. Arthur's widow, Jeanne Moutoussamy-Ashe, received two standing ovations as she welcomed the crowd. She was especially pleased to see all the new, young players who were there that day.

One such player—Venus Williams—won her first match with a 119-mile-per-hour serve on her final point and went all the way to the finals. It was Williams's first U. S. Open, and her performance gave her a taste of victory. It was, in a sense, a victory for Arthur Ashe, too.

SOURCES

 1 Arthur Ashe, *Off the Court* (New York: New American Library, 1981), 175.

 7 Arthur Ashe and Arnold Rampersad, *Days of Grace* (New York: Alfred A. Knopf, 1993), 6.

21 Ashe, *Off the Court*, 21.

22 Ibid., 35.

23 Ibid., 36.

25 Ibid., 35.

29 Ibid., 41.

30 Ibid., 37.

31 Ibid., 25.

32 Ibid., 26.

35 Ashe and Rampersad, *Days of Grace*, 281.

35 Ibid.

39 Ashe and Rampersad, *Days of Grace*, 5.

40 Ashe and Rampersad, *Days of Grace*, 6.

41 Ashe, *Off the Court*, 47.

44 Ashe, *Off the Court*, 81.

50–51 Ibid., 63.

53 Ibid., 68, 69.

55–56 Ibid., 82, 84.

58 Allison Danzig, *The Greatest Sports Stories from The New York Times* (New York: A. S. Barnes and Co., 1951), 527.

64 Ashe and Rampersad, *Days of Grace*, 61, 116.

64 Ashe, *Off the Court*, 89.

69 Ibid., 95.

74 Ibid., 99, 102.

82 Ibid., 112.

80 Ibid., 109.

83 Ibid., 114, 115.

84 Ashe and Rampersad, *Days of Grace*, 302.

89 Ibid., 105.

90 Ibid., 106.

95 Charlie Rose, "A Conversation with Arthur Ashe," PBS-TV, September 2, 1996.
100 Carol Jenkins quoted in *People* magazine, February 22, 1993, 70.
103 Ashe and Rampersad, *Days of Grace*, 75.
104 Ibid., 81.
108–109 Ashe, *Off the Court*, 214.
111 Ashe and Rampersad, *Days of Grace*, 54.
112 Ibid., 252.
115 Ibid., 124.
118 Ashe and Rampersad, *Days of Grace*, 279–280.
119 Frank Deford, "Lessons from a Friend," *Newsweek*, February 22, 1993, 60.

PHOTO ACKNOWLEDGMENTS

Photos were reproduced with the permission of: AP/Wide World Photos, pp. 2, 39, 59, 62, 82, 99, 101, 102, 108, 113, 114, 116, 120; ALLSPORT/HULTON DEUTSCH, pp. 6, 94; UPI/Corbis-Bettmann, pp. 8, 9, 38, 42, 60, 65, 74, 75, 81, 86, 91, 103; Reuters/Corbis-Bettmann, pp. 11, 111, 119; Corbis-Bettmann, pp. 12, 15, 51, 78, 85, 96 (top and bottom), 97, 106; Schomberg Center for Research in Black Culture, p. 16; Richmond Times Dispatch, pp. 18, 20, 23, 33, 34, 71; International Tennis Hall of Fame, Newport, Rhode Island, pp. 24, 26, 68, 70, 72, 79, 98; Lynchburg News and Advance, p. 29; © Carol L. Newsom, pp. 36, 121; UCLA Photography, pp. 44, 46, 49, 54, 57; ALLSPORT USA/Ken Levine, p. 50; ALLSPORT USA/Tony Duffy, p. 92; ALLSPORT USA, p. 110; Flip Schulke, p. 67; Independent Picture Service, p. 77; American Lutheran Church, p. 88; R. L. Watson, p. 89; Caroline Lazo, p. 105. Front cover photograph © Archive Photos/SAGA/Frank Capri. Back cover photograph by Richmond Times Dispatch.

BIBLIOGRAPHY

Ashe, Arthur. A Hard *Road to Glory: A History of the African American Athlete.* 3 vols. New York: Warner Books, 1988.

Ashe, Arthur, and Clifford Gewecke Jr. *Advantage Ashe.* New York: Coward-McCann, 1967.

Ashe, Arthur and Arnold Rampersad. *Days of Grace: A Memoir.* New York: Alfred A. Knopf, 1993.

Ashe, Arthur with Neil Amdur. *Off the Court.* New York: New American Library, 1981.

Ashe, Arthur with Frank Deford. *Arthur Ashe: Portrait in Motion.* Boston: Houghton Mifflin, 1975.

Danzig, Allison. *The Greatest Sports Stories from The New York Times.* New York: A. S. Barnes and Co., 1951.

Little, Alan. *Wimbledon Men: A Hundred Championships 1877–1986.* London: Wimbledon Lawn Tennis Association, 1986.

PERIODICALS

Ashe, Arthur. "What Does the Future Hold for Blacks in Sports?" *Ebony,* August, 1992, 102.

Ayres, B. Drummond Jr. "Ashe Returns to City He Disowned in Youth," *The New York Times,* May 8, 1992, A8.

Baker, Peter. "Ashe's Widow Joins Critics of Statue Site," *Washington Post,* January 3, 1996, D1.

Barker, Karlyn. "Arthur Ashe Jailed in Apartheid Protest," *Washington Post,* January 12, 1985, B1.

Berkow, Ira. "A Monumental Man on Monument Avenue," *The New York Times,* August 28, 1995, B7.

Deford, Frank. "Lessons from a Friend," *Newsweek,* February 22, 1993, 60–61.

Huzinec, Mary, et al. "Man of Grace and Glory," *People,* February 22, 1993, 68–72.

Lamb, David. "A Question of Honor, History, and Equality," *Los Angeles Times,* March 11, 1996, E1.

Lloyd, Barbara. "Arthur Ashe Is Inducted into Hall of Fame," *The*

New York Times, July 14, 1985, SP7.

Quindlen, Anna. "Journalism 2001," *The New York Times,* April 12, 1992, E21.

Rhoden, William C. "Arthur Ashe: A Hero in Word and Deed," *The New York Times,* February 7, 1993, S1.

Sebastian, Pamela. "Arthur Ashe AIDS Foundation To Close after Creating $1 Million Endowment," *Wall Street Journal,* January 13, 1995, B9.

Steinberg, Jacques. "Guiding Hand of Arthur Ashe Is Remembered," *The New York Times,* February 8, 1993, A1.

Trescott, Jacqueline. "Ashe's Steady Partner, Jeanne Moutoussamy-Ashe, Determined in the Face of His Illness," *Washington Post,* May 29, 1992, D1.

Vecsey, George. "America Loses a Hero and a Gentle Man," *The New York Times,* February 8, 1993, B7.

Verdon, Lexie. "Boycotting South Africa," *Washington Post,* September 13, 1983, B1.

Weil, Martin. "Tennis Legend Arthur Ashe Dies at 49," *Washington Post,* February 7, 1993, A1.

Wolf, David. "Arthur—King of the Courts," *Life,* September 20, 1968, 30–35.

Zonana, Victor F. "Ashe Case Raises Fame Vs. Privacy Debate, *Los Angeles Times,* April 10, 1992, A26.

INDEX

ABOUT THE AUTHOR

Caroline Lazo has written numerous biographies of men and women who have broken down barriers of race, religion, and gender to achieve equality for struggling peoples around the world. Her works include *Gloria Steinem,* also published by Lerner Publications Company.

Ms. Lazo was born and raised in Minneapolis, Minnesota. She graduated from the University of Minnesota. She pursued her interests in international relations at the University of Oslo, Norway.